Athos

Sword fights, adventure, spying, chivalry: The Three Musketeers *will appeal to everyone who likes a fast-paced and thrilling story. Here is the first adventure of those three brave men, with their companion D'Artagnan who was more daring than any of them.*

THE THREE MUSKETEERS

Alexandre Dumas

retold in simple language
by Joan Cameron

with illustrations by Frank Humphris

Ladybird Books Loughborough

The Three Musketeers

One morning in April, 1625, the little French town of Meung was in a state of great excitement. In those times, fighting was common in France. The King fought the ambitious Cardinal Richelieu, who wanted to be as powerful as the King himself. Noble families fought among themselves, and Spain was always ready to wage war. Few days passed without trouble in some town or another.

On this particular day, a crowd had gathered outside the Inn. The cause of all the stir was the arrival of a young man. He was riding the oddest horse the townspeople had ever seen. It looked so comical that many of

them wanted to laugh. Only the length of the sword at the young man's side, and the proud gleam in his eye, stopped them from doing so.

The young man was called D'Artagnan. He was on his way to Paris, where he hoped to fulfil his dearest wish — to become a King's Musketeer. His father had given him a letter to Monsieur de Tréville, an old friend who was now Captain of the Musketeers.

As he dismounted, D'Artagnan caught sight of a gentleman with a scar on his temple sitting at the Inn's open window. He was talking to two others. They were laughing, and D'Artagnan was sure they were laughing at him.

This was more than he could bear.

'Tell me what you are laughing at, sir,' he called furiously. 'Then we will laugh together.'

'I was not speaking to you, sir.'

'Are you laughing at me?' demanded D'Artagnan, drawing his sword.

'I laugh as I please,' the man replied, turning away and re-appearing in the doorway.

Angrily, D'Artagnan lunged at him. Startled, the other man drew his sword. At the same moment, the innkeeper and several onlookers, anxious to prevent a fight, fell upon D'Artagnan. He was knocked senseless in the struggle, and carried indoors for attention.

When the innkeeper returned, the gentleman with the scar asked how the young man was.

'He will soon recover,' replied the innkeeper. 'I don't know who he is, sir, but he carries a letter to Monsieur de Tréville in Paris.'

'Indeed!' The other man became alert. 'I would like to know what is in that letter. He is a nuisance, this young man. Please make out my bill. I am leaving. I must meet Milady and I do not wish her to be seen by him.'

Soon afterwards, partly recovered, D'Artagnan limped into the courtyard. The first thing he saw was the gentleman, talking to a beautiful young woman in a carriage.

'What are the Cardinal's orders?' she was asking.

'You must return at once to England. Keep watch on the Duke of Buckingham. As soon as he leaves London, inform the Cardinal. I am returning to Paris.'

D'Artagnan rushed forward.

'Stand and fight, sir!' he demanded. 'Would you dare run away from me in front of a woman?'

Seeing her companion lay his hand on his sword, Milady touched his arm.

'Remember, delay could ruin our plans.'

'You're right,' he agreed. 'Go on your way, and I will go on mine.'

With that, the carriage moved off, the driver cracking his whip. The gentleman jumped on his horse and galloped away in the opposite direction.

'Coward!' D'Artagnan called after him, but he was gone.

D'Artagnan was ready to leave for Paris when he found his letter to Monsieur de Tréville was missing.

'My letter! It's gone!'

The innkeeper hastened to protect himself.

'That gentleman must have taken it, sir. He showed great interest in it.'

The letter seemed to be gone for good. All D'Artagnan could do was hope Monsieur de Tréville would see him without it.

Monsieur de Tréville was a close friend of King Louis XIII. In those troubled times the ruler of France needed this brave man at his side. Tréville led the King's Musketeers, a band of bold men dedicated to protect their King.

Cardinal Richelieu, who had almost as much power in the country as the King himself, also had his own men — the Cardinal's Guards. He and the King constantly boasted to one another about their men's courage, and secretly encouraged them to fight.

Monsieur de Tréville's headquarters was always full of Musketeers. When D'Artagnan arrived, he made his way through them, his heart beating with excitement. He was allowed in to see Monsieur de Tréville, but had

to wait. The Captain was scolding three of his men.

'Athos! Porthos! Aramis! I hear you were fighting in the streets and were arrested by the Cardinal's Guards. This will not do!'

'But they attacked us!' they protested. 'We fought back, and escaped.'

'The Cardinal didn't tell me that,' murmured Monsieur de Tréville. 'However, I will not allow my men to risk their lives for nothing. The King needs his brave Musketeers. Now you may go, and I will see this young man.'

Eagerly, D'Artagnan explained who he was. Monsieur de Tréville smiled.

'I liked your father. What can I do for his son?'

D'Artagnan explained that he had come to Paris to join the Musketeers.

'That won't be possible right away,' the Captain told him. 'I'm afraid no one becomes a Musketeer without first serving in a less important regiment. But I will do this for you. I will send you to the Royal Academy, where you will learn horsemanship and swordsmanship. Let me know how you are getting on.'

Thanking Monsieur de Tréville, D'Artagnan left, excited over his good luck. On the way out he had the misfortune to meet, one after the other, the three Musketeers he had seen in the Captain's room. Still smarting from the scolding they had received, they took offence easily. D'Artagnan upset them all so much that he found himself facing three duels. The first was to be with Athos at noon, the second with Porthos at one o'clock, and the third with Aramis at two!

Dismayed, D'Artagnan said to himself: 'I can't draw back. But at least if I am killed, I shall be killed by a Musketeer!'

D'Artagnan knew no one in Paris. He went to meet Athos alone, determined to fight well. When Athos arrived, he brought the other two Musketeers with him. All three were astonished to see that it was the same young man they were to fight, one after the other.

'Now that you are here, gentlemen,' D'Artagnan said, 'I wish to apologise.'

At the word 'apologise' he saw contempt appear in their faces. They thought him a coward. His hot blood rose.

'You don't understand! I apologise only in case I am unable to fight all three of you. Monsieur Athos has the right to kill me first. And now – on guard!'

With the most gallant air possible, D'Artagnan drew his sword. Athos had just drawn his when a company of the Cardinal's Guards appeared.

'Sheathe your swords!' called Porthos and Aramis together, but it was too late.

'Fighting, Musketeers?' cried one of the Guards mockingly. 'You know that isn't allowed. Put up your swords. You're under arrest!'

'Never!' called the three Musketeers. 'There may only be three of us, but we will fight.'

'You are wrong — there are four of us,' D'Artagnan said quietly. 'Try me.'

'What's your name, brave fellow?' asked Athos.

'D'Artagnan, monsieur.'

'Well, then, Athos, Porthos, Aramis, and D'Artagnan, forward!'

Swords clashed and men cried out as they fought fiercely to and fro. The Cardinal's Guards were also good swordsmen, but at last they were beaten off. Afterwards, the four returned to Monsieur de Tréville's headquarters, arm in arm.

D'Artagnan's heart swelled with pride.

'I am not yet a Musketeer, but at least I must be an apprentice.'

The affair caused a great fuss. Monsieur de Tréville scolded his Musketeers in public, but congratulated them in private. The King heard of it and was so impressed by D'Artagnan's bravery that he placed him as a cadet in the Guards of Monsieur d'Essart.

From then on D'Artagnan and the three Musketeers were the greatest of friends. D'Artagnan learned about life in Paris, and about the Court of King Louis XIII and the lovely Queen Anne. He was happy, and looked forward to the day when he too would become a Musketeer.

One day, while D'Artagnan was resting in his lodgings, his landlord, Monsieur Bonacieux, came upstairs to see him.

'I have heard you are a brave young man, D'Artagnan. I need help. Constance, my wife, has been kidnapped!'

'Kidnapped?'

'My wife is seamstress to the Queen,' Monsieur Bonacieux explained. 'She is more than that. She is one of the few people the Queen can trust.'

D'Artagnan had heard a great deal about the Queen. She was a lonely woman. Everyone knew that the King no longer loved her. The Cardinal had once cared for her, but she had rejected him. Now he plotted jealously against her. The English Duke of Buckingham, a powerful man in the government of his own country, had fallen deeply in love with her. But England and France were not friendly.

Monsieur Bonacieux sighed.

'I think my wife was kidnapped to see if she would tell the Queen's secrets. Only the other day she told me the Queen is frightened. She thinks the Cardinal has written to Buckingham in her name, to lure him to Paris and into a trap.'

'You think the Cardinal has taken your wife?'

'I fear so,' replied Monsieur Bonacieux. 'One of his men was seen when she was carried off. He was a gentleman with a scar on his temple.'

D'Artagnan started up.

'That sounds like the man I met at Meung!' he exclaimed.

'Will you help me?' begged Monsieur Bonacieux. 'You are always with the Musketeers, who are enemies of the Cardinal. I thought you and your friends, while helping the Queen, would be glad to spoil his plans.'

'I will do what I can,' D'Artagnan agreed. 'And if the man who carried off your wife is the man I think he is, I will be revenged for what happened to me at Meung!'

D'Artagnan lost no time in telling Athos, Porthos and Aramis of the disappearance of Constance Bonacieux.

'This woman is in trouble because of her loyalty,' he told them. 'I am also anxious about the Queen's safety.'

'I have heard people say she loves our enemies, the Spanish and the English,' said Athos.

'Spain is her own country,' D'Artagnan reminded him. 'It is only natural that she should love the Spanish. As for the English — only one Englishman is involved, Buckingham,

the King of England's chief minister. Now the
Cardinal and his men seem to be using his
admiration for the Queen in some wicked
plot.'

The Cardinal was their true enemy, the
friends agreed. If they could spoil his plans, it
would be worth risking their heads. The
missing Constance Bonacieux was the key to
the whole intrigue. She must be found, and
they would do it together.

The four men stretched out their hands and
shouted in one voice:

'All for one, and one for all!'

23

D'Artagnan's task was to keep watch on Monsieur Bonacieux's apartments from his own room on the upper floor. Monsieur Bonacieux had been arrested, and the Cardinal's Guards were using his house as a trap. Anyone arriving there was taken away for questioning to see what they knew of the Queen's affairs.

Late one night, D'Artagnan heard cries from downstairs. Realising it was a woman's voice, he drew his sword and rushed to the rescue. The woman was Constance Bonacieux herself! She had escaped, and returned home. The Cardinal's men had followed her, but surprised by D'Artagnan's attack, they ran away.

"Thank you for saving me!" cried Constance Bonacieux. "Now I must go — there is something I have to do for the Queen."

A few hours later, D'Artagnan was astonished to see her in a dark street. She was with a Musketeer who looked like Aramis. What were they doing? D'Artagnan hurried up to speak to them, and found the man was a stranger, disguised in a Musketeer's uniform. He was the English Duke of Buckingham! Constance Bonacieux was taking him to a secret meeting at the Louvre with the Queen.

'Please don't give us away,' Madame Bonacieux begged. 'You can ruin us all.'

D'Artagnan shook the Duke's hand.

'I will make sure you reach the Louvre safely.'

At the Louvre, Madame Bonacieux led the Duke into a quiet drawing room. Buckingham had come to Paris in answer to a message, supposed to be from the Queen. On his arrival in the city, he had learned the message was a trap, set by the Cardinal.

Although the English Duke knew he was in danger, he refused to return to London without seeing the Queen. He waited, unafraid, while the trusted Constance Bonacieux brought her mistress to see him.

Buckingham turned as the Queen came into the room, her lovely face pale. She implored the Duke to return to England and safety. She made him promise not to see her secretly again. It was too dangerous.

'Come as an ambassador, with guards to defend you,' she said. 'Then I will know you are safe.'

'Very well,' Buckingham agreed. 'Please give me something of yours, perhaps a ring or a chain. I will wear it to remember you.'

Queen Anne thrust a rosewood casket into his hands.

'Take this, and go, before it is too late!'

Unknown to the Queen, Cardinal Richelieu was soon to know about her secret meeting with Buckingham. The news was brought to him by the Comte de Rochefort, the very man who had so annoyed D'Artagnan at Meung. An agent of the Cardinal, he had placed a spy in the Queen's household.

'The Queen and Buckingham have met,' he told the Cardinal. 'He has already left for England.'

'Then our plan has failed,' said the Cardinal, angrily.

'The Queen gave Buckingham a gift,' Rochefort went on. 'It was a box containing the twelve diamond studs the King gave her on her birthday.'

'Well, well!' The Cardinal smiled suddenly. 'All is not lost.'

He sat down and wrote a letter. Closing it with his seal, he sent for a servant.

'Take this at once to London,' he ordered. 'Stop for no one.'

The letter said:

'Milady de Winter — be at the first Ball Buckingham attends. He will wear on his doublet twelve diamond studs. Cut off two of these. As soon as you have them, inform me.'

King Louis XIII was next to know about Buckingham's visit, for the Cardinal told him himself. The King demanded to know why Buckingham had come.

'No doubt to conspire with your enemies,' replied the Cardinal.

'He came to see the Queen!' insisted the King, furiously.

'I am unwilling to think so,' said the Cardinal. He knew how suspicious the King was of his wife. 'But I have heard she cried this morning, and spent the day writing letters.'

'I must have these letters!' cried the King.

He immediately sent the Chancellor to search the Queen's rooms, but the only letters he found were to the Queen's own brother. They attacked the Cardinal's power in France, but did not mention Buckingham. The King was delighted.

'I was wrong, Cardinal,' he admitted. 'The Queen is true to me.'

The Cardinal bowed his head.

'Perhaps you should do something to please her, sire. Give a Ball. The Queen loves dancing. It would be a chance for her to wear those beautiful diamonds you gave her for her birthday.'

The Queen was surprised and happy when the King told her about the Ball. She asked eagerly when it was to be held. The King told her the Cardinal would arrange everything. Every day for more than a week, however, the Cardinal made some excuse for not setting the date.

On the eighth day he received a letter from Milady de Winter in London. It read: 'I have them. Please send money and I will bring them to Paris.'

The Cardinal knew that Milady could be there in ten to twelve days. Content that his plans were going well, he spoke to the King about the Ball.

'Today is September 20th. I have arranged that the Ball will take place in the Hôtel de Ville on October 3rd. And do not forget, sire, to remind the Queen to wear the diamond studs!'

The Queen was delighted when Louis told her the Ball would soon take place. But her delight soon turned to shock.

'I wish you to appear in your most beautiful gown,' he told her, 'wearing the diamond studs I gave you for your birthday.'

The Queen stared at the King.

'When is the Ball?' she asked faintly.

'The Cardinal has arranged it for October 3rd,' replied the King. At the sound of that name, Queen Anne grew pale.

'Was it also his idea that I should wear the diamond studs?'

'What if it was?' demanded the King. 'Do I ask too much?'

The Queen shook her head. 'No, sire.'

'Then you will appear as I ask?'

'Yes, sire.'

Once the King had gone, Queen Anne sank into a chair in despair.

'I am lost,' she murmured. 'The Cardinal must know everything. What am I to do?'

And she began to weep.

'Don't cry, your Majesty.'

The Queen turned sharply around, for she thought she was alone. It was Constance Bonacieux, who had heard everything.

'Don't be afraid,' she told the Queen. 'We will get those diamonds back in time for the Ball!'

Constance Bonacieux knew her husband would not help. The Cardinal had released him, and given him money. He was now a Cardinal's man. There was one person who could help — D'Artagnan. She told him what had happened, first swearing him to secrecy.

'I will go to London at once,' he told her.

Realising not a moment was to be lost, D'Artagnan went to see Monsieur de Tréville. He asked if he could arrange leave of absence for him.

'I must go to London,' he explained. 'I am on a secret mission for the Queen.'

Monsieur de Tréville looked sharply at the eager young man.

'Will anyone try to prevent you?'

'The Cardinal would if he knew,' D'Artagnan admitted.

'Then you must not go alone,' said Monsieur de Tréville. 'Athos, Porthos and Aramis will go with you. Then surely one of you at least will get through to London.'

'Thank you,' D'Artagnan said, gratefully.

Athos, Porthos and Aramis were as excited as D'Artagnan himself when he explained their mission.

The four adventurers left Paris at two o'clock in the morning. As long as it remained dark, they kept silent. In spite of themselves, they expected ambushes on every side. With the sunrise, their spirits rose.

All went well until they arrived at Chantilly, early in the morning. They stopped at an inn for breakfast. After the meal, the first sign of danger appeared. A stranger who had shared their table called on Porthos to drink the Cardinal's health. Porthos agreed, if the other would then drink the health of the King. The stranger cried that he would drink to no one but the Cardinal. A bitter argument followed. Leaving Porthos to settle it, the others hurried on their way.

They had travelled for several hours when they came upon men mending the road. As they drew level, the workmen drew out concealed muskets.

'It's an ambush!' cried D'Artagnan. 'Ride on!'

They spurred their horses forward, but Aramis was wounded in the shoulder. He was able to travel only a little further. Athos and D'Artagnan had to leave him to be looked after at a village inn.

Only D'Artagnan and Athos were left. They rode on. At nightfall they took a room at Amiens. The night passed quietly enough, but when Athos went to pay the bill in the morning, the landlord accused him of using forged money. Four armed men rushed in. They had obviously been waiting.

'Ride on, D'Artagnan!' shouted Athos, drawing his sword.

D'Artagnan did not need to be told twice. He galloped on. At length, his horse exhausted, he reached Calais, the port for ships bound for England. He ran on to the quay. There, a travel-weary gentleman was telling a ship's captain that he must go to England. The ship was ready to sail, the captain explained, but the Cardinal had just issued an order. No ship was to leave without his permission.

'I already have it,' the gentleman said, showing a paper. 'Will you take me?'

The captain agreed, but insisted that the pass had to be signed by the Port Governor. Hearing this, D'Artagnan hurried away and waited amongst some trees for the gentleman to come back with the signed pass. He had to have the Cardinal's pass. Naturally, the man refused to give it up, and D'Artagnan had to fight him for it. They fought fiercely for some time before the man at last gave in and handed over the precious piece of paper.

Breathing hard, D'Artagnan thrust the pass into his pocket and went to find a ship to take him to England.

The ship D'Artagnan chose had scarcely left harbour when a cannon boomed out. The port had been closed. He had only just been in time. Worn out, D'Artagnan slept while the ship sailed across the Channel. In the morning, he watched eagerly while the vessel dropped anchor in Dover. Soon he was on his way to London.

The young Frenchman knew no English, but he had the Duke of Buckingham's name written on a piece of paper. He was soon directed to the Duke's home, for everyone in London knew him. When he heard that

D'Artagnan had come, the Duke saw him at once. He remembered him from their meeting in the dark streets of Paris.

His face became grave when D'Artagnan told him of the Queen's danger.

'We must return the diamond studs to her. Louis must not find out she gave them to me!' he exclaimed. He unlocked the box in which they lay, with a key from a chain he wore round his neck. As he lifted the diamonds out, he gave a startled cry.

'Two of them are missing!'

'Can you have lost them, my lord?'
D'Artagnan asked anxiously.

'They have been stolen,' the Duke replied
grimly. He showed D'Artagnan where the
ribbon holding the two missing studs had been
cut.

'Wait!' said the Duke. 'I remember now. I
wore them only once, at a Ball in London.
Milady de Winter was there. She has never
liked me, but she was unusually friendly. I
wondered why. She must have taken them.
She must be an agent of the Cardinal.'

44

He paced up and down, thinking. The Ball, D'Artagnan told him, was in five days' time. If Queen Anne appeared with two of the diamond studs missing, the King's anger would be terrible. The Cardinal would have succeeded. The Duke stopped suddenly and turned to the young Frenchman.

'Five days — that's all the time we need!' he exclaimed. 'I know what we must do.'

Buckingham sent for his secretary, and issued an immediate order. No ships were to sail for France, for he believed Milady de Winter was still in London. Such was his importance in the government that the order was carried out without question.

Next the Duke called for his jeweller, and showed him the set of diamond studs. He promised the man he would pay him well to make two studs exactly like them. They must be finished within two days, and made so that no one could tell the new from the old. The jeweller agreed, and hurried away to start work.

'We are not beaten, D'Artagnan!' cried the Duke.

Two days later the new studs were ready. The Duke and D'Artagnan examined them carefully. They had been so well made it was impossible to tell they were not part of the original set. Now D'Artagnan could leave for France.

As his ship left Dover, he thought he saw Milady de Winter aboard one of the vessels which had not been allowed to leave port. His ship passed so quickly he had little more than a glimpse of her. Once across the Channel he set off for Paris as fast as he could.

Paris was full of talk about the Ball, at which the King and Queen would lead the dancing. More than a week had been spent in preparing the Hôtel de Ville, with flowers and hundreds of candles. The King arrived to the cheers of the watching crowds. Soon afterwards the Queen also entered the ballroom. The Cardinal watched from behind a curtain. A smile of triumph came to his lips. She was not wearing the diamond studs. He was quick to point this out to the King.

'Madame, why are you not wearing the diamond studs?' the King demanded.

The Queen looked round, and saw the Cardinal.

'Sire, I was afraid they would be damaged in this crowd. I will send for them.'

While the Queen waited with her ladies in a side room, the Cardinal gave the King the box containing the two studs Milady de Winter had stolen from Buckingham.

'Ask the Queen where these two diamond studs have come from,' he suggested.

His triumph turned to rage when the Queen re-appeared, proudly wearing the set of diamond studs. All twelve were there!

'What does this mean?' the King asked,
puzzled, pointing to the two the Cardinal had
given him. The Cardinal thought quickly.

'I wished her Majesty to have them as a present. Not daring to offer them myself, I adopted this plan.'

'I must thank you, your Eminence,' said the Queen. Her smile showed she had understood the Cardinal's plot. 'I am sure these two must have cost you as much as all the others cost the King.'

D'Artagnan had watched the Queen's triumph over the Cardinal. Apart from the King, the Cardinal and the Queen herself, he was the only one in the crowded ballroom who had understood what was happening.

Later, the Queen sent for him. She thanked him, and gave him a diamond ring. D'Artagnan put it on and returned to the gaiety of the Ball. He was well content. He was in favour with the King and Monsieur de Tréville, and had helped his Queen when she most needed it. Above all, he had gained the friendship of three brave men, Athos, Porthos and Aramis. One day, he too would be a Musketeer, just like them.

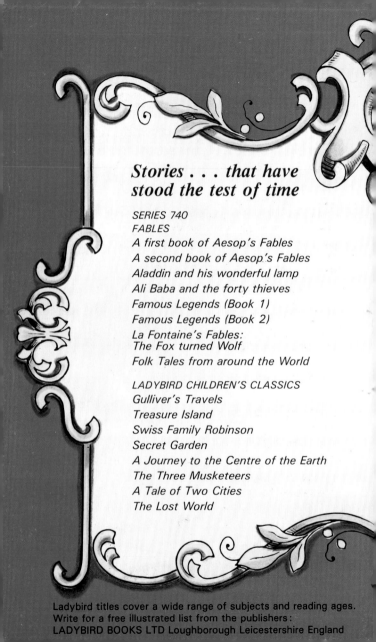

Stories . . . that have stood the test of time

Ladybird titles cover a wide range of subjects and reading ages.
Write for a free illustrated list from the publishers:
LADYBIRD BOOKS LTD Loughborough Leicestershire England